This book belongs to

....

Quarto is the authority on a wide range of topics.

Quarto educates, entertains and enriches the lives of our readers—enthusiasts and lovers of hands-on living.

www.quartoknows.com

© 2018 Quarto Publishing plc

First published in 2018 by QED Publishing,
an imprint of The Quarto Group.
The Old Brewery, 6 Blundell Street,
London N7 9BH, United Kingdom.
T (0)20 7700 6700 F (0)20 7700 8066
www.QuartoKnows.com

All rights reserved. No part of this publication may be reproduced, stored in a retrieval system, or transmitted in any form or by any means, electronic, mechanical, photocopying, recording, or otherwise, without the prior permission of the publisher, nor be otherwise circulated in any form of binding or cover other than that in which it is published and without a similar condition being imposed on the subsequent purchaser.

A catalogue record for this book is available from the British Library.

ISBN 978-1-91241-380-5

Based on the original story by Caroline Castle
and Claire Shorrock
Author of adapted text: Katie Woolley
Series Editor: Joyce Bentley
Series Designer: Sarah Peden

Manufactured in Dongguan, China TL042018

9 8 7 6 5 4 3 2 1

MIX
Paper from
responsible sources
FSC® C104723
FSC
www.fsc.org

Reading Gems

SNAP!

QED

In the hot sunshine on the banks of a river, animals played in the trees and insects buzzed through the air.

Suddenly, there was a loud noise and a crocodile pulled herself out of the water to warm up on the riverbank.

"Ahhh, a crocodile!" called Milly Meerkat.

"Quick, climb up high," said Betty Baboon.

Snip! Snap! Snip! Snap! laughed the happy crocodile.

Callie Croc swished her long spiky tail and sang a little song to all the animals on the riverbank:

Look at me, I am so fine!
With these big sharp teeth of mine!
Sixty of them go snip, snip, snip!
Come too close and I'll nip, nip, nip!

All the animals sped away as fast as they could. None of them wanted to be eaten by a big, snappy crocodile.

Betty Baboon had climbed up the tallest tree she could find. She shivered and she shook as she held on tightly to her baby. Then, she sang him a little song:

Listen to your mama
and stay close by.
For I love you
more than the mountain high.

Milly Meerkat had run into the bushes where she hugged her three baby meerkats.
She sang them a little song, too:

Never wander off
but keep me in your sight.
For I love you
more than the stars shine bright.

The mother lion is the queen of all the animals but even she was afraid of the big, snapping crocodile.

Lily Lion had found her bouncing cubs hiding in the tall grass. She sang them a little song:

Don't stray too far
from my side.
For I love you
more than the ocean is wide.

Back on the riverbank, the crocodile heard a tapping and a rumbling. Underneath her tummy, the ground began to move.

She started to dig, dig, dig.

There, safely tucked under the sand, were her crocodile eggs. They were all wriggling and jiggling as they made a tap, tap, tapping sound.

One by one, little baby crocodiles tapped their way out of the eggs with their teeth.

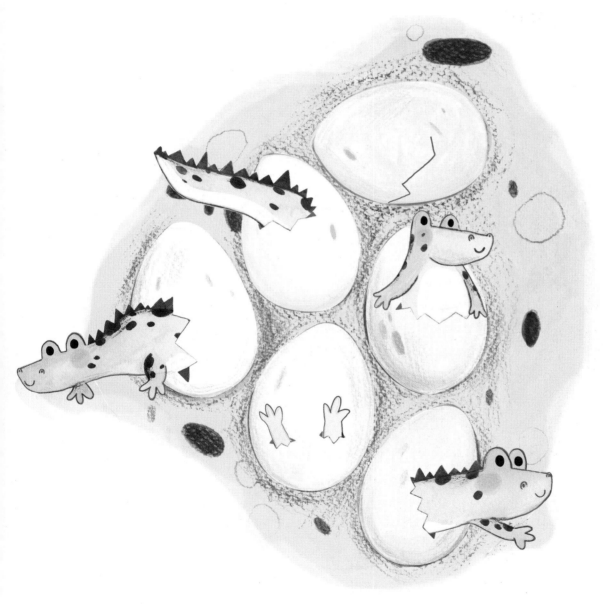

One, two, three, four, five, six tiny crocodiles!

Soon there were lots and lots of crocodiles all snapping their teeth as they scampered about under the hot sun.

Callie Croc smiled and swished her huge tail.

"Hooray, hooray! Twenty-three baby crocs born today!" she snapped.

All of the tapping and snapping had made such a noise that the other animals had come to see what had been going on. They watched as Callie Croc popped each baby into her large mouth.

"Do something," said Lily Lion.
"Callie Croc is eating her babies!"

The animals didn't know what to do. Callie Croc was too big and they were too small.

But, Callie Croc had a secret. Gently, she waddled to the edge of the water and opened her mouth.

One by one, her baby crocodiles popped out into the water. They were soon swimming happily in the river.

The newest mum on the riverbank swam and played with her babies all day long. As they grew tired, she scooped them up onto her tummy and sang a song:

Stay close by me
and no tears will you weep.
For I love you
more than the river is deep.

The other animals listened to Callie Croc sing her babies to sleep.

They understood the crocodile mummy might be big but she wasn't scary. She loved her babies like the rest of them.

And so, as night fell, all the animals slept soundly by the light of the moon.

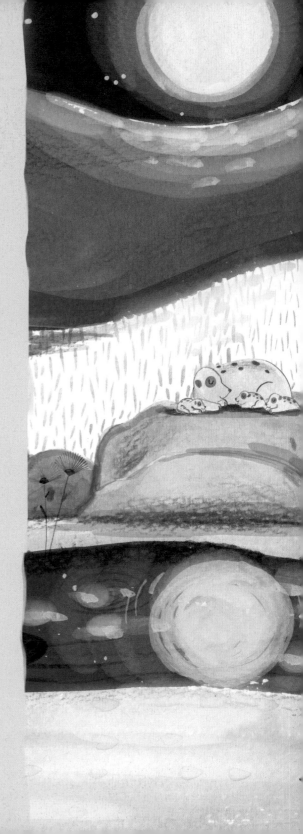

Story Words

baby

Betty Baboon

bushes

Callie Croc

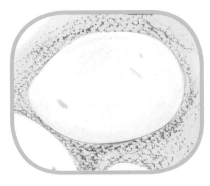

eggs

grass

insects

Lily Lion

Milly Meerkat

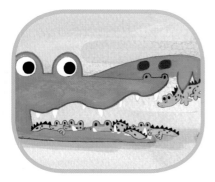

mouth

mum

river

riverbank

swimming

tree

water

Let's Talk About Snap!

Look carefully at the book cover.

Count all the animals you can see.

The story is all about the animals looking after their babies.

What ways do they look after their children?

Look back at the pictures and read the story again to help you.

This story is all about animals in Africa. Look at a map of the world.

Can you find Africa?
Where do you live?

Crocodiles have green, scaly skin. Describe the appearance of a lion, a meerkat and a baboon.

What do the animals all have in common with each other?

The mums all sing songs about how much they love their children. Have a go at making up a song yourself.

Did you like the ending of the story?

What do you think happened next?

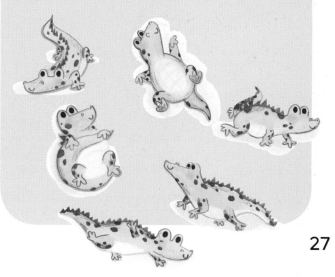

Fun and Games

Look at the words at the top of the page.
Find and circle each word five times
in the box below.

mouth   tree   grass   bush

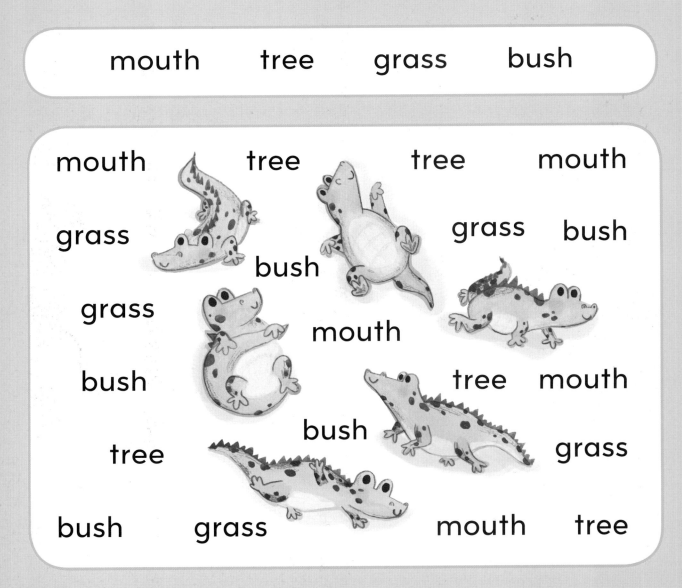

mouth   tree   tree   mouth

grass   grass   bush

          bush

grass

          mouth

bush

               tree   mouth

          bush

tree   grass

bush   grass   mouth   tree

The story has lots of rhyming words.
Can you match up these rhyming pairs?

snip

side

wide

deep

high

nip

weep

by

Your Turn

Now that you have read the story,
have a go at telling it in your own words.
Use the pictures below to help you.

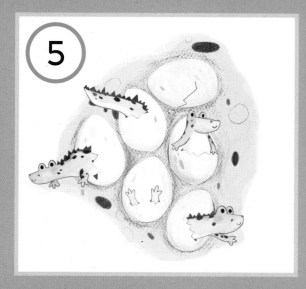

GET TO KNOW READING GEMS

Reading Gems is a series of books that has been written for children who are learning to read. The books have been created in consultation with a literacy specialist.

The books fit into four levels, with each level getting more challenging as a child's confidence and reading ability grows. The simple text and fun illustrations provide gradual, structured practice of reading. Most importantly, these books are good stories that are fun to read!

Level 1 is for children who are taking their first steps into reading. Story themes and subjects are familiar to young children, and there is lots of repetition to build reading confidence.

Level 2 is for children who have taken their first reading steps and are becoming readers. Story themes are still familiar but sentences are a bit longer, as children begin to tackle more challenging vocabulary.

Level 3 is for children who are developing as readers. Stories and subjects are varied, and more descriptive words are introduced.

Level 4 is for readers who are rapidly growing in reading confidence and independence. There is less repetition on the page, broader themes are explored and plot lines straddle multiple pages.

Snap! is about the different ways animal mothers care for their young. It explores themes of accepting differences and love.

Level 4

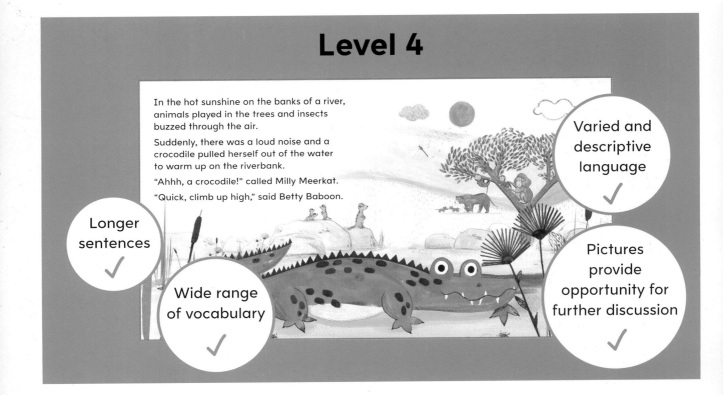

In the hot sunshine on the banks of a river, animals played in the trees and insects buzzed through the air.

Suddenly, there was a loud noise and a crocodile pulled herself out of the water to warm up on the riverbank.

"Ahhh, a crocodile!" called Milly Meerkat.

"Quick, climb up high," said Betty Baboon.

Longer sentences ✓

Wide range of vocabulary ✓

Varied and descriptive language ✓

Pictures provide opportunity for further discussion ✓